The boys and girls of St. Ciarán's N.S. Clonmacnois who were Sammy and Riley's first
fans and encouraged their tricks and antics to come to life!
For Sheeba

The Adventures of Super Sammy and Smiley Riley

Amy Heraghty

Double Trouble

AUSTIN MACAULEY PUBLISHERS™

LONDON * CAMBRIDGE * NEW YORK * SHARJAH

The Adventures of Super Sammy and Smiley Riley!

Sammy and Riley are two furry friends.
Come enter their world where the fun never ends.
Freddy, their human, is a kind-hearted boy,
full of love, and fun, and most of all, joy.
He loves his two buddies with all of his heart.
And now it is time for the chaos to start...
Sammy is the oldest of this mischievous motley crew.
And Riley, he's the cuter, younger one of the two.
Together combined, they're one of a kind.
Sammy's really clever, he's a mastermind.
When he sees an opportunity for fun to be had,
in the blink of an eye, he's snout deep in something bad.

Riley gets fed up of his brother's crazy crimes.
He's witnessed Sammy tell lies too many times.

Sam reckons his little brother is just a cunning little pest...

But perhaps Riley's not that innocent.
After all, he learns from the best!

The Arrival of a Rival!

One afternoon while Sammy enjoyed a well-earned rest,
he was paid a little visit by a certain little pest.
After a morning full of mischief, Sammy really needed a nap.
But his snooze was interrupted by this cheeky little chap.
At first Sam didn't realise this visitor would stay.
For when he learned this truth, there would be hell to pay!

"Why did they get another?
Wasn't I enough?
I'll be good from now on, I won't indulge in all things rough.
I'll shine the wood floor,
I'll lick the tiles clean,
I'll even put the dirty laundry into the washing machine.
I'll make the bed every morning,
I'll put my toys away.
But please I'm begging you,
don't let that little squirt stay!"
But Sammy's plea came too late.
Riley would stay – it was fate!

Riley entered his new home making lots of noise.
Was there really enough room there for these two mischievous boys?
Sammy decided that if Riley's here to stay...
"I'll see if he's worthy, there's a big price to pay.
I'll frighten little Riley far far away..."
Then and there, Sammy devised a cunning plan
to trick little Riley as often as he can...

The Fart Attack!

One fine day, Riley was startled, he really didn't know what to do.
He had a pain in his tummy, he just wanted his mummy, and he felt like
he needed to do a... "Number two!"

When all of a sudden, his bum did explode.
And soon out of it, a funny smell flowed.

Although then and there, the pain seemed to lighten,
but poor little Riley it sure did frighten.
Fear took a grip of his heart as he wondered what caused that to start.
He was worried and nervous because never before had he ever done such a fart!

Sammy, of course, saw the look on his face,
when after his own tail, Riley started to chase.
Sniffing and whinging, and wondering why
his bum had made such a **CRACK**.
Sammy smiled a cheeky dubious grin,
"Little brother, you're having a **FART ATTACK!**"

"A fart attack?" said Riley with fear.
"Oh no! This cannot be!
I exercise every day and always eat healthily.
This cannot be happening to me!"

"Oh, but it is," replied sneaky Sam,
"I've seen this kind of illness before.
It starts with your tum
and ends with your bum,
and soon you'll be dead on the floor!"

"Goodness gracious!" shrieked Riley, trembling with nerves,
"But surely there must be a cure?"

"Well…" Sammy started with eyes open wide,
"You could try to eat some manure!
Manure, that's right, that's the only cure!"

"Manure?" Riley asked,
"Where can I get some? Will you tell me please where it is found?"

"That's simple, young chap, we don't need a map.
There's plenty of it on the ground!
In the farmyard where Daisy the cow does reside,
brown bundles of joy you will find.
For this chocolate mousse (or sometimes brown juice)
is delivered from Daisy's behind."

Without a second thought, the two boys dashed
to the farmyard to find some manure.
Riley, still worried, turned to Sam and said,
"Thank you for finding the cure."
In moments, the two had found some delicious poo.
And Riley no longer could wait.
"PARPPP!" he let out another cracker,
"Hurry up or it'll be too late!"

Sammy seemed so genuinely concerned to make sure his brother ate just enough.
"Thank you, sweet Sam," said Riley again with a mouthful
of some gooey brown stuff.

"How much do I need to make sure I survive?
How much of the cure should I take?"

"Three dozen mouthfuls and lick your paws clean to ensure the attack you do break.
If you don't eat enough, your insides will spurt out your bum and land on the floor.
That's right, you'll explode from the inside out.
Then, little Riley, you'll be no more!"
So Riley did just as his big brother advised and thanked him for saving his life.
And Sammy just smiled a cheeky wide grin after causing all this mayhem and strife!

Is this just the beginning of Sammy's tricks and traps?
Life is full of fun with these funny furry chaps!

Underwear Everywhere!

Freddy awoke one morning with a thud and a thump.
There was something quite strange about his rump.
He raced up the hall with a song and a dance.
"Ma!" he called out, "Where's my underpants?"

"I don't know, dear, now please cover your rear.
Have you checked every drawer and looked under your bed?"

"Yes, Mother dear, I've checked them all," he said.
Now Fred was going red...

"Of course they pointed the finger at me!
I get the blame for everything, you see.
Not little Riley, he's so cute and smiley.
He causes the trouble; he sets me up!
Oh, what an arrogant mischievous pup.
Now clearly, you see, it wasn't me.
For at the time of the crime, my eyes were closed and off to sleep I dozed."

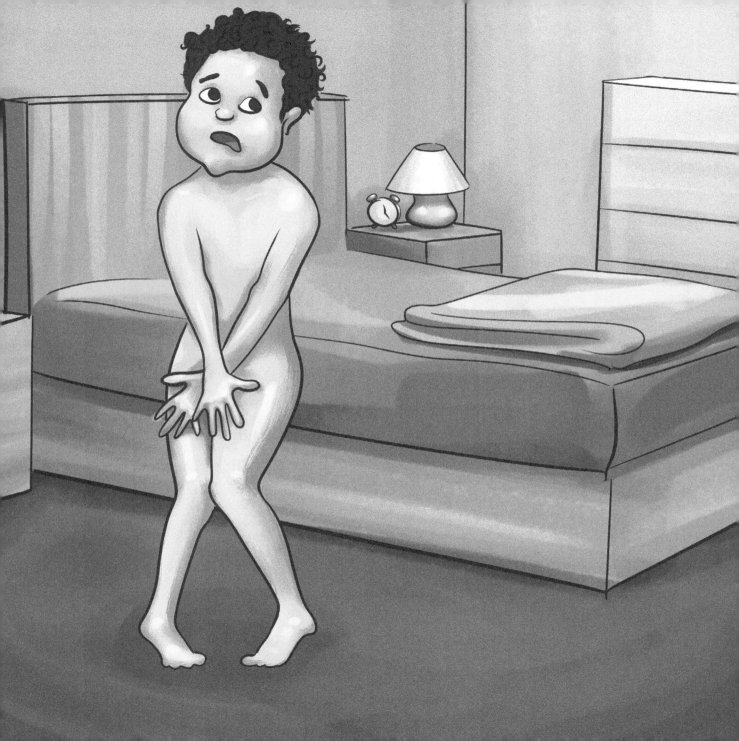

But Riley just has to rain on Sam's glory.
Remember, there's always two sides to a story...

Here's Riley's reply to Sammy's big lie:
"Cover your ears, he'll reduce you to tears.
Don't believe a word, this is completely absurd.
That story's not true – he's lying to you!
I can't remain mute, I'm not only cute, I'll tell you the truth.
The truth is that when our human's asleep,
into his bedroom sneaky Sammy does creep.
With eyes open wide, he's hungry for fun.
'I'll take underpants this time, but only the one.'"
But Sammy, he never knows when to stop.
Not one underpants, he took the whole lot.
Spotty ones, stripy ones, green ones and blue,
ones with footballs and superheroes and ones that smelt like...
BRAND NEW! (Did **YOU** say **POO**? Who knew!)

Poor Freddy was worried, he was shaking with fear,
for now he had nothing to cover his rear.
He searched the whole house, no underpants to find.
You see, Sammy's a genius, he's a mastermind.
He knew trouble would come if Freddy found out.
The disappeared underpants were once in Sammy's mouth!
"Sammy?" said Freddy with a hint of suspicion.

"Don't look at me!" snarled Sammy, "I was sleeping in the kitchen."
"Steady now, Freddy, I do beg your pardon!"
But poor Freddy didn't know yet,
he hid them in the... garden!

MOOve Over!

One fine evening in the month of May,
Sammy enjoyed a rustle around in a bale of hay.
While Freddy had to count every cow on the farm,
Sammy saw an opportunity to cause a little harm.
You see, Daisy the cow was a stubborn old heifer,
and Sammy didn't like her since the moment he met her.
But when Daisy's involved, it is sure to be a battle.
This stubborn old girl refuses to move.
And if Sammy draws near her, she'll raise up her hoof.

This time Daisy decided no way would she budge,
despite Sammy's efforts to push, shove, nudge, nudge.
In the blink of an eye and the swoosh of a tail,
poor Daisy leapt over the highest bale.
With a bum more pink than usual, she started to flinch
from the pain inflicted by Sammy's sharp pinch!
"That's what happens!" said Sam with a satisfied smirk,
"If you don't cooperate, it just won't work!"

"You pinched my bum, you sneaky mutt.
You clenched your teeth into my butt!
You'll pay for this, just wait and see.
This isn't the last you'll see of me
and oh-so sorry you will be!"

An Udder Problem!

Later that night, the cattle came back.
They waited for midnight to plan their attack,
in through the gates and onto the lawn,
where they would remain 'til the break of the dawn.

Sammy howled, shaking with fear,
"They're coming for me!
They're drawing near!"

Daisy and company mooed and mooed.
Raising their tails, they...
CHEWED AND CHEWED (who said **POOED**!!?).
Grazing the lawn in the midst of the night were two dozen Frisians.
Oh what a sight!

"Oh Sammy," a voice called, "You're not so brave now?
Are you really scared of an old dairy cow?"
Daisy gasped wryly as she stomped her feet.
"Aaaaah!" she exclaimed. "Revenge is sweet!"

"You've chased us and ordered us from field to shed.
You've pinched our bottoms and ruined our bed!
You've pushed us around the place with your head.
You've hid our food so we wouldn't get fed.
You even pretended one of us was dead!
Now it's your turn to suffer instead!
We've had enough! This is payback
for every single one of your cheeky attacks!
We'll give you a taste of your own medicine
so you know how we lived in fear.
Surrender now, Sammy, it's time to bend over,
it's our turn to pinch your posterior!
First on our list, we will mess up your bed exactly like you did to ours.
We'll dig it all up, roll around like a pup,
and sprinkle with warm urine showers!"

Sammy stood shaking, holding his breath, for he knew he was in deep trouble.
When all of a sudden, a cheeky head popped up from under some rubble.
"Never fear, Smiley Riley is here, I'm here to save my big brother!"
Without hesitation, Riley faced those Frisians swinging from udder to udder!

With a pinch and a clinch, and a nip and a rip, Riley, full of courage and strength, warned the two dozen Frisians of brotherly love and soon back to the farm yard they went.

Sammy watched in shock, as out of the gate
the cattle quickly and quietly scattered.
He smiled as he thanked his now-favourite pest
and realised brotherly love is all that matters.

Maybe having a little brother isn't so bad.
Having Riley by his side made him ever-so glad.
Sammy was sure things felt different this time.
He not only had a brother, but a partner in crime!

Copyright © Amy Heraghty (2020)

A CIP catalogue record for this title is available from the British Library.

ISBN 9781788482721 (Paperback)
ISBN 9781788482738 (Hardback)
ISBN 9781528954310 (ePub e-book)

www.austinmacauley.com

First Published (2020)
Austin Macauley Publishers Ltd
25 Canada Square
Canary Wharf
London
E14 5LQ

Amy Heraghty (B.Ed., M.Ed.) is a children's author who spent most of her childhood and adult years living in the land of make-believe! After spending a number of years sharing her love for high-quality children's literature with parents and most importantly with many children in her primary school classroom, she completed a master's in education, specialising in children's emergent literacy development. She believes that the essence of children's storybooks not only lies in vivid details and enticing imagery, but in the storyteller's voice. Oh, and with a little imagination, anything is possible!

CPSIA information can be obtained
at www.ICGtesting.com
Printed in the USA
LVHW071454310321
683077LV00020B/1371

9 781788 482721